READING CORNER

PHONICS

The Old Tin Bath

Written by
Clare De Marco

Illustrated by
Martin Remphry

Practising long vowel phonemes,
trisyllabic words and tricky words

First published in 2010 by
Franklin Watts
338 Euston Road
London NW1 3BH

Franklin Watts Australia
Hachette Children's Books
Level 17/207 Kent Street
Sydney NSW 2000

Text © Clare De Marco 2010
Illustration © Martin Remphry 2010

A CIP catalogue record for this book is available from the British Library.

ISBN: 978 0 7496 9171 4 (hbk)
ISBN: 978 0 7496 9180 6 (pbk)

Series Editor: Jackie Hamley
Series Advisors: Dr Barrie Wade,
 Dr Hilary Minns
Series Designer: Jonathan Hair

Printed in China

There is a puzzle at the end of this book.
Here are the answers for you to check later!

The matching words are:
heat meat, meet, sheet
shark bark, lark, park, stark
shower flour, flower, hour
water daughter, quarter

"I don't need a bath!"

shouted Amy.

"You should have a bath," said Mum.

4

5

Next door, Mrs Smith laughed. "When I was a child, we had an old tin bath."

"A tin bath?" said Amy

7

"Yes," said Mrs Smith. "And we could only have a bath once a week on a Friday afternoon."

"My brother thought we should
only have a bath once a month."

"Yuck!" said Amy.

"My father would heat up some water. My brother and I would go first, and then my mother. My father went last."

"In the same water?" asked Amy.

"Oh, yes," said Mrs Smith.

15

"My brother told me there were sharks in the water. He was very silly. How can a shark fit in a bath?"

"But when I was little,
I got very scared!"

"That wasn't nice," said Amy.

"No," said Mrs Smith. "I didn't like my bath. But now I do. There's lots of hot water. There's even a power shower!"

"The old tin bath is now full of flowers," said Mrs Smith.

23

"It's so little!" said Amy.

"Yes," said Mrs Smith. "You're lucky to have your bath!"

"I am," laughed Amy.

"Time to have a bath now!"

28

Puzzle Time!

Match the words that rhyme
to the pictures.

heat

park

flower

daughter

shark

meet

flour

lark

shower

sheet

bark

quarter

meat

stark

hour

water

See page 2 for answers.

Notes for parents and teachers

READING CORNER PHONICS has been structured to provide maximum support for children learning to read through synthetic phonics. The stories are designed for independent reading but may also be used by adults for sharing with young children.

The teaching of early reading through synthetic phonics focuses on the 44 sounds in the English language, and how these sounds correspond to their written form in the 26 letters of the alphabet. Carefully controlled vocabulary makes these books accessible for children at different stages of phonics teaching, progressing from simple CVC (consonant-vowel-consonant) words such as "top" (t-o-p) to trisyllabic words such as "messenger" (mess-en-ger). READING CORNER PHONICS allows children to read words in context, and also provides visual clues and repetition to further support their reading. These books will help develop the all important confidence in the new reader, and encourage a love of reading that will last a lifetime!

If you are reading this book with a child, here are a few tips:

1. Talk about the story before you start reading. Look at the cover and the title. What might the story be about? Why might the child like it?

2. Encourage the child to reread the story, and to retell the story in their own words, using the illustrations to remind them what has happened.

3. Discuss the story and see if the child can relate it to their own experience, or perhaps compare it to another story they know.

4. Give praise! Small mistakes need not always be corrected. If a child is stuck on a word, ask them to try and sound it out and then blend it together again, or model this yourself. For example "wish" w-i-sh "wish".

READING CORNER PHONICS covers two grades of synthetic phonics teaching, with three levels at each grade. Each level has a certain number of words per story, indicated by the number of bars on the spine of the book:

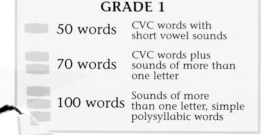

GRADE 1

	50 words	CVC words with short vowel sounds
	70 words	CVC words plus sounds of more than one letter
	100 words	Sounds of more than one letter, simple polysyllabic words

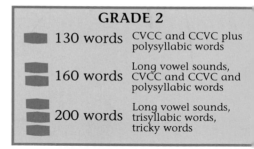

GRADE 2

	130 words	CVCC and CCVC plus polysyllabic words
	160 words	Long vowel sounds, CVCC and CCVC and polysyllabic words
	200 words	Long vowel sounds, trisyllabic words, tricky words